Copyright © 2006 by NordSüd Verlag AG, Gossau Zürich, Switzerland
First published in Switzerland under the title *Annas Islandpony, Der erste Ausritt*
English translation copyright © 2006 by North-South Books Inc., New York.

First published in the United States, Great Britain, Canada, Australia, and New Zealand in 2006 by North-South
Books Inc., an imprint of NordSüd Verlag AG, Gossau Zürich, Switzerland. Distributed in the United States by
North-South Books Inc., New York.

Library of Congress Cataloging-in-Publication Data is available.
A CIP catalogue record for this book is available from The British Library.

ISBN-13: 978-0-7358-2081-4 / ISBN-10: 0-7358-2081-3 (trade edition)
10 9 8 7 6 5 4 3 2 1

Printed in Belgium

Krista Ruepp
Anna's Prince

ILLUSTRATED BY

Ulrike Heyne

Translated by J. Alison James

NORTHSOUTH
BOOKS

New York / London

The herd of horses galloped across the farmyard. Anna opened the gate to the large pasture behind the house. The horses flooded through, and within moments their noses were buried deep in the spring grass. After a long winter, the fresh grass tasted especially delicious.

It was spring, which was when they broke the four-year-olds. The young horses had to learn to carry riders. This year was special for Anna, because her horse had turned four and she would finally be able to ride him.

"Catch Prince and bring him in," called Anna's father. Prince belonged to Anna. He didn't need catching. He welcomed her with a loud whinny and came running. He tugged at her sweater. He loved Anna. Anna clipped on his halter and led him into the riding circle.

Her father had a long lead line in his hands and a saddle and bridle lay in the grass.

Carefully, Anna rubbed the bridle up against Prince's head. Then she held the bit flat in her hand and let him feel it with his mouth. While she was doing that, her father snapped the lead line onto the bridle.

Anna led Prince a few times around the ring. As they walked, she stroked him, so he grew comfortable with the strange gear on his head.

She stopped. Her father lifted the saddle and settled it on Prince's back, then tightened up the girth before Prince noticed what was happening.

Prince didn't like that. He pulled suddenly at the rope and ran off, bucking wildly. He wanted to throw off the saddle, but he couldn't. It was buckled on too well.

"Whoa there, you're okay," said Anna gently. Soon she managed to calm her horse.

When Prince had gotten used to the saddle, Anna's father pulled it off and set it aside.

"Now I'll lift you up, and you just lie on him," Anna's father said. "He needs to get used to your weight on his back."

She stood next to the horse. Her father hefted her up like a small sack of flour and laid her on Prince.

Prince held still and looked back over his shoulder at the girl.

When Anna looked up, she saw their neighbor's son, Sean, gallop across the meadow on his white horse. "Oh, Prince," whispered Anna, "soon I'll be riding you just like that."

Anna liked Sean.

"Come on down now, Anna," her father said. "Prince has learned enough for today."

"Good boy, Prince," Anna praised. She took off his bridle and brought him back to the young horses in the meadow.

Anna ran to the riding ring the next morning, but her father was already there and had Prince all saddled up.

"Papa, can I ride him today?" she asked, out of breath.

"We'll try it," said her father. He helped Anna mount. Slowly Prince took one wobbly step forward, then two, then three. The horse had to find his balance with a rider on his back. It wasn't easy.

"Whoa, gently now, Prince," Anna said. It was strange for Prince to have Anna's voice suddenly come from above. He could hear her, but he couldn't see her. He looked left and right, and then still not seeing Anna, Prince began to gallop. Anna dug her hands into his bushy mane. Just stay on, she thought.

Prince calmed down after a while. He snorted and then slowed down to a walk.

"Well done, Anna," said her father. "Shall we call it quits for today?" Anna agreed.

Sean had seen them. He came over. "Nice job, Anna," he said. Anna smiled at Sean and jumped off Prince.

"Can I ride Prince alone tomorrow, Papa?"

Her father considered. "If Sean helps us, we could try. Do you have time tomorrow, Sean?"

"Sure," answered Sean, patting Prince on the neck.

Before going to bed, Anna went out to the meadow once more to see Prince.

"Tomorrow I'll ride you properly for the first time," she said. The rays of the evening sun glittered like red blades of light over the sea. Anna listened to the crunching noises the horses made grazing in the grass. The scent was fresh. Prince gave her a nudge, and she laughed.

That night, Anna had a dream. She flew on Prince's back along a sandy beach. She rode by rivers and waterfalls, all the way to a sparkling lake.

Dark snowcapped mountains shimmered in the distance, and Prince stopped to drink the clear lake water. He drank greedily, slurping loudly and splashing all over . . .

Anna awoke. It was raining and windy.
Down in the farmyard, her father was ready,
with his own horse and Prince already saddled up.
Sean was waiting, too, mounted on his white horse.

They set off. Anna and Prince rode between the two older
horses. They would help to keep him calm and under control.

The three horses pranced in the cool weather. They were snorting
with excitement. Papa kept a tight grip on the lead line. Anna let the
reins go loose. She trusted Prince.

When they had left the farm behind, her father released the lead line.
Calm and confident, Anna rode smoothly next to the two of them. They
reached the edge of a small lake where a camper had set up a tent. Two
swans swam on the glittering waves.

Suddenly, the swans unfolded their enormous wings and took off, splashing the water and honking. At the same moment, a burst of wind blew under the red tent and it flapped with a loud *clap-snap*.

The sudden noise spooked Prince. Anna pulled on the reins and clamped her legs tightly to the saddle, but that tickled Prince's sensitive belly and he began to buck.

Prince sprang to the side. Anna tried to keep her grip, but Prince bucked again, and she lost her balance and landed in the grass. "Prince!" cried Anna. Her legs felt like pudding, as she jumped up. Luckily she wasn't hurt, but Prince had given her a big fright. Prince stopped at the edge of the lake. His flanks trembled. Then he came slowly back to Anna. He nudged her, leaned his head against her face, and stood quietly.

"You want me to ride you again?" asked Anna.

Prince snorted.

"Good. Let's try again."

"Everything okay, Anna?" asked her father. Anna didn't say anything. She just mounted her horse. She was still a bit weak at the knees.

"Well done," praised Papa. Then the three of them rode on, with Prince cantering calmly in the middle. Anna was still a little shaken, but she didn't want to let it show in front of Sean.

When they got back to the farm, Anna turned to Sean. "I'd like to ride again tomorrow," she said. "Do you want to come?"

"Great!" said Sean, enthusiastically. "We can ride down to the sea."

The next day, Anna and Sean rode all the way down to the sea. Laughing, they galloped on the glittering beach. Anna was proud of her horse. Prince trusted his rider, and she trusted him. She knew they would have many adventures together.